WOODEN SHIP

WOODEN SHIP

written, designed, and illustrated by
Jan Adkins

WoodenBoat Books, Brooklin, Maine

Copyright 2004 by Jan Adkins

Published by WoodenBoat Publications Inc
Naskeag Road, PO Box 78
Brooklin, Maine 04616 USA
www.woodenboat.com

ISBN: 0-937822-85-X

Originally published by Houghton Mifflin Co, 1978

Written and illustrated by Jan Adkins

Printed in Canada by Friesens

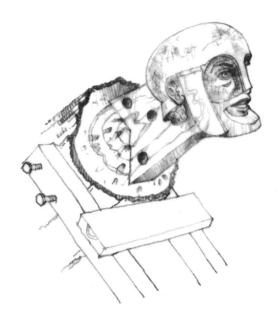

for

SAMUEL ULYSSES ADKINS

The author gratefully emphasizes the help and advice of Mystic Seaport in Mystic, Connecticut, which provided indispensible research, photographs and plans, Willets D. Ansel of the Mystic Seaport Restoration Shop, whose knowledge and brief monograph on shipbuilding were most valuable, Bert Bigelow, a wise Friend without whose counsel I could not have begun or completed *Ulysses,* and John Swain Carter, ship's carpenter, singer of songs, a glad spirit. Thank you.

Two brothers of New Bedford, Massachusetts, John and Albert Ingalls, are wealthy men from the selling of whale oil and whalebone. Their whale oil lights lamps all over the United States, and their whalebone shapes the corseted figures of stylish ladies in ballrooms everywhere. They manage the counting house of Ingalls & Ingalls on Johnnycake Hill, and from their windows they can look down on the thick tangle of rigging that webs the edge of the harbor. Among the freighters, colliers, revenue cutters, and coasting schooners they can see three of their six whalers: *Edward B. Stetson, The Honorable Albert Bigelow,* and the *Double Eagle*. They know that their brig *Sally* is in the dockyard at San Francisco shipping a new mast. Good word from the whaleship *Simplicity* has just been received from a returning vessel. She is nearly full! of oil and bone, almost ready to return from the Indian Ocean. The brig *Thea* has not been reported for seven months, but they do not worry, for in a voyage that may well last five years these lapses of communication are not uncommon. Further, the brothers Ingalls belong to the Religious Society of Friends, the Quakers. They are

gentle men for whom the will of God is a sure and purposeful force, controlling alike their destiny and the destiny of the *Thea*. A bountiful God, as real and immediate to them as the oaken floor they walk on, has provided the stuff of which to make floors and whaleships, an ocean full of whales, and a market for their oil and bone. To these gentlemen, wealth is not a badge of distinction but a burden of responsibility and an opportunity to glorify His name. Increasing that wealth is a duty and a covenant.

Today they are discussing the advantages of adding another vessel to their fleet. Pros and cons discussed, cash investment weighed against sure returns, the temper of the times accounted for, they decide: yes, a full-rigged whaleship to be built in Fairhaven, across the river from where they stand.

John consults his watch (oiled, as all fine watches are, with sperm oil) and notes that they yet have time to bespeak Mr. Percival Knowlton, master shipbuilder. As they stride into the street they talk excitedly. They are men of God and men of business, and they are happy men.

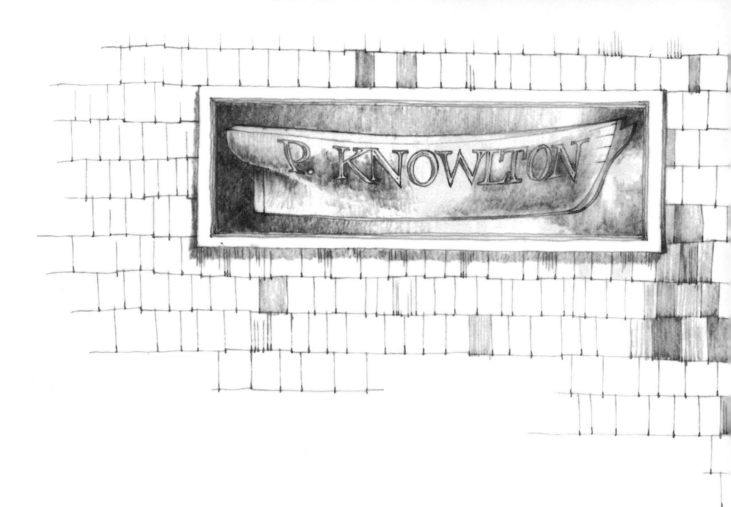

How does a ship take its look and form? Not all at once, not like a painting takes its look or a sculpture takes its form. A ship is too big, too complex. Every line in its forest of rigging is a strength or a weakness, every curve or smooth in its hull has something to say about the ship's way with the sea. Knowing how to build a ship is a skill that began six thousand years ago, a skill passed from one man to another, each man making his contribution or adding the example of his mistakes. Shipbuilding began with little, delicate coastal boats and grew to the complicated skill of building great warships, merchantmen, and world-circling passage makers.

Designing a ship is a great responsibility. The lives of the men who sail her out to the storms depend on the designer. The fortunes of the men who have her built depend on the designer too—the fortunes of the brothers Ingalls as they visit Mr. Knowlton of Fairhaven. Mr. Knowlton is not a member of the Society of Friends, nor of any church anyone knows of. He smokes long black cigars brought from Honduras on the packet boat, he swears and drinks and worse, but the brothers trust him. He has steady, unwavering eyes, and if his speech *is* peppery, it is calm and honest.

They sit before Mr. Knowlton's stove and describe their needs: a whaling ship of about 300 tons, about 100 feet along the deck, with a good beam of 27 feet (her width) and about 16 feet for draft (how deep she will lie in the water). Yes, Mr. Knowlton agrees that a good beam is a comfortable quality in a whaleship. Yes, he can present plans and estimates in a month and if all is well the building can begin in the spring, yes.

The brothers Ingalls take their leave; it has been an exciting day for them. Mr. Knowlton's head begins to bubble with the needs of his new project . . . the design of the hull, the lumber, the hardware, the workmen, the time of year. His responsibility begins.

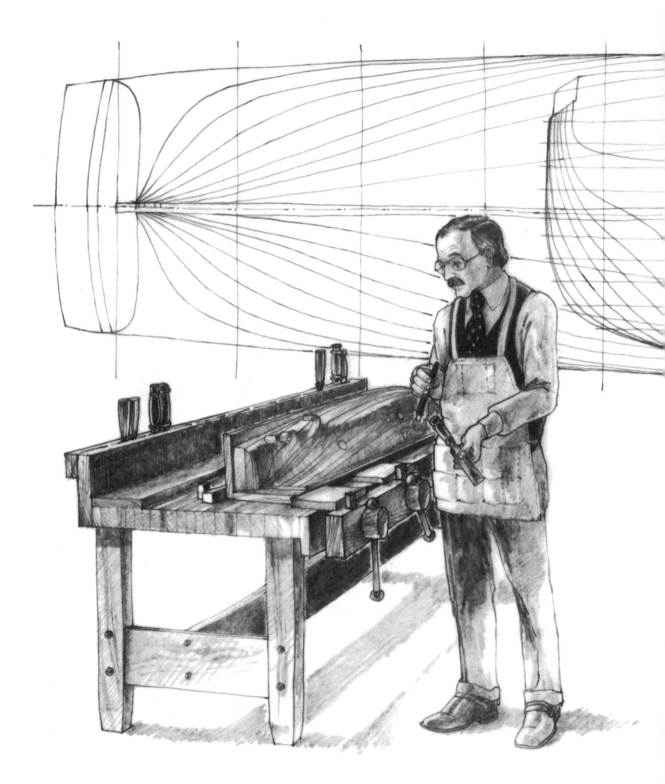

10   *the half model*

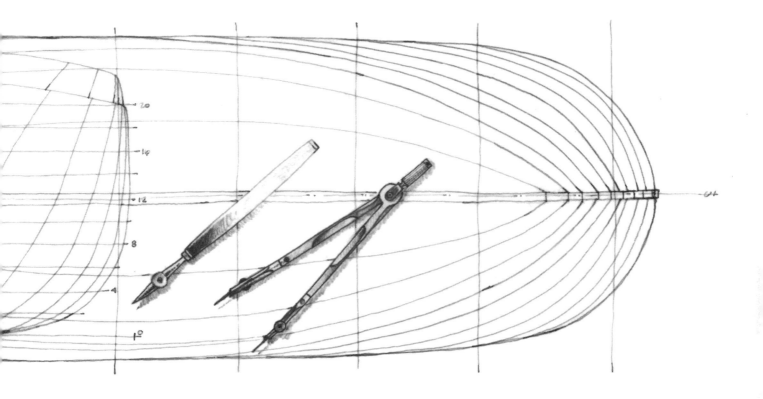

   The ship begins. The first way anyone will see the ship is as a small model, or really a *half-model*. Mr. Knowlton lays up layers of wood held in place with wooden pins and he carves away at this wooden layer cake to find the shape of the hull in it. It is a way to see the real shape of the hull, to see the water cut by the bow and eased aside, to picture the water flowing around it, to see the bulk of the cargo hold under the water, the flow rushing back to meet the rudder, the *wake* (the waves shouldered up by the ship's movement) smoothing away under the stern.

   The half-model is also a tool, a way of making precise drawings of the ship. When Mr. Knowlton is satisfied with the shape (he will work on it for a week and look at it for weeks afterward), he will unstack the layers of wood and trace around them. When all the lines are set down together he—and his workmen, and the apprentices learning from him, and even the brothers Ingalls—may see the gentle curves of the hull. Together, those curves are called the *lines* of a ship, and they are the plans for its building.

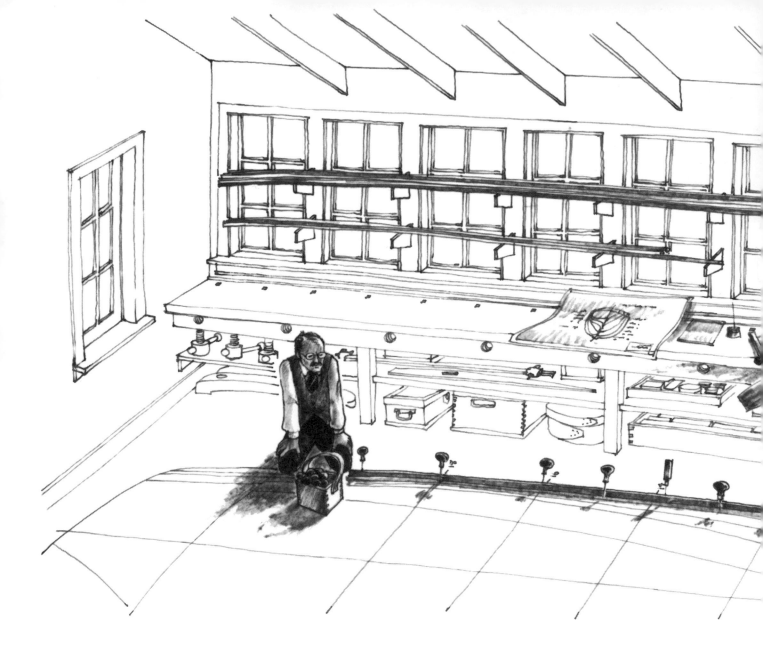

Now the plans are to be *lofted*; the small-scale drawings of the lines will be en-larged to full size and laid out on the smooth floor of a wide room, the loft (attic) of a large shed or warehouse. Most masterbuilders were finicky and secretive about the way they lofted their plans; they taught their methods only to their apprentices and the workmen who helped them, the *boss-liners*, and they jealously guarded these methods and special tools and mathematics from everyone else.

When the lines are laid down, they cut wooden patterns for each of the ship's ribs and timbers. It is now toward the end of winter and the *hewers,* the men who will

cut and shape the trees to fit these patterns, are anxious to begin their work before the spring thaw sends sap up into the oaks and tamaracks, for sap-wet wood will twist and warp and set the ship out of true. This is not a boat to last one season.

Off they go at last, small teams of men in sleds and wagons drawn by thick-limbed draft horses, up into the woods of Acushnet and Mattapoisett, Tinkamtown and Rochester, to find the big trees with just the right curve for that number three rib, and a good clear piece for the apron. The ship is lying with the patterns carried in their sleighs, and it is standing quietly in the trees of the forest.

14   *laying the keel*

The keel is the ship's backbone, her center line, her focus of strength. It is early spring, the yardmen still wear gloves and mufflers, and the keel is being laid. It is almost a hundred feet long and as straight as a tight string, built up out of hewn oak logs 16 inches square, and shoed along the bottom with a 3-inch sole of tamarack. The logs are fastened along their length with scarf joints, diagonal cuts that even out the load. They are fastened through their 3-foot depth with iron bolts driven through undersized holes with sledgehammers and bent over on the top. The sole that will protect the keel from scraping is fastened with pegs, so that it may be replaced when it is worn.

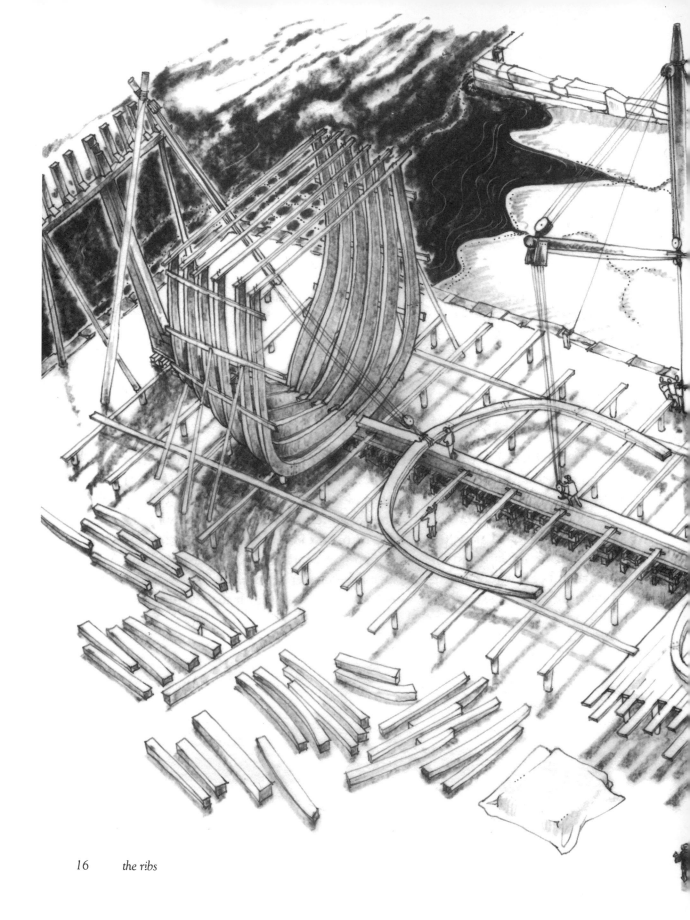

16   *the ribs*

Like a great, clumsy Chinese puzzle the ship is fitted together. Forward, a platform is built on the keel and on it the *timbers* (ribs) are assembled. Each timber is *double-sawn:* since no onepiece of timber can make the whole rib, many pieces (called *futtocks*) are halved together so that the butt ends join beside a solid length. The pieces that span the keel are called *floors,* and they are notched so that the planking, the skin of the ship, will bed into the keel, into a notch called the *rabbet.*

When a timber is complete and measured and trued, it is slid aft on runners and raised into place with gin poles and block and tackle and winter sweat. It is kept from sagging out of shape by *crossbands* spiked across its top, and held into the march of the other ribs with long planks called *ribbands.*

The shape of the hull is clear now. The last of the *cant frames* is being lifted into place. These are timbers that are not continuous across the keel but fit into the stem forward and into the deadwood aft. (The *deadwood* is the built-up fin that continues back to the rudder under the rising stern.)

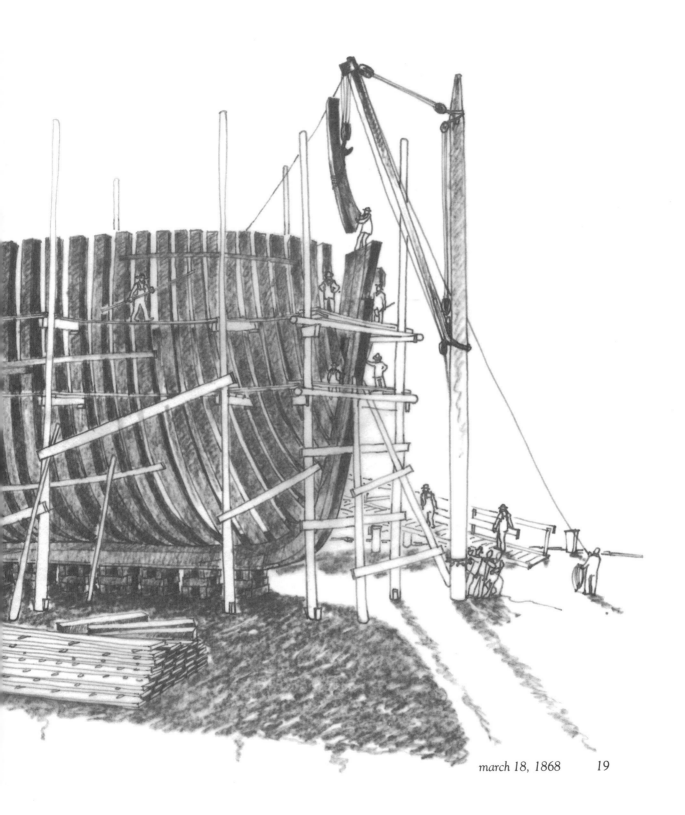

the keelson

Over the timbers is fitted the *keelson*. Drift pins are driven through keelson, timbers, and into the keel, clamping them all together to make an oak backbone almost 6 feet deep.

A late winter rain, and work on the hull is slowed. George Fearing is rolling oakum into strands for the job of caulking to come later. Oakum is loose hemp fiber bound with tar. He rolls it with his hand against a scrap of canvas thrown over his knee. It's a mindless, pleasant job near the warmth of the stove, among the tools.

auger

centerhead   spar marking gauge

J. S. CARTER

broad xe

splice fonn

rigger's vise & tools

caulker's stool & tools

april 30, 1868   23

The skin of the ship is oak and white pine, hard and thick. Every plank is set to the ribs with care, its edges planed to meet its brothers square and flat, outside corners beveled to make it easy to wedge in the caulking. Under every *strake* (band of planking) the curving ribs are marked and trimmed with a lipped adz to make a flat, true-bearing surface. The men who mark and trim are called *dubbers*, and they are wonderfully delicate with their big, razor-edged adzes. Planks *amidship* (at the middle of the ship) lie easy with a simple curve to follow; they are *shored in* with posts and wedges and fastened with locust pins called *trunnels* (for "tree nails"). Each end shares half a rib, and a plank is trunnel-fastened four times at each rib. Forward and aft the curves are complex and more pronounced. For that work the big kettles start to boil, shooting steam into the long steaming boxes where stiff planks lie sweating out their stubbornness. As the box is cracked open a white plume of steam rushes up and Knowlton's men pluck a hot plank out with leather gloves and hooks. They rush it, still whippy with the heat and damp, up to the ribs and clamp it down to its curve before it stiffens again. The trunnels, almost twenty thousand of them, give the ship a rash of stubbly texture before the dubbers trim them flush.

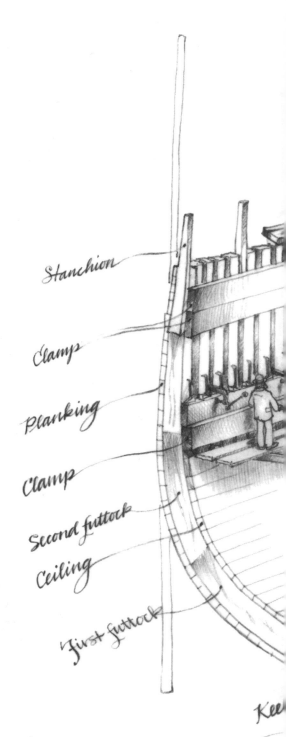

Stanchion

Clamp

Planking

Clamp

Second futtock

Ceiling

First futtock

Keel

floor

Keel
Fals
Sho

A wooden ship has an inner skin and an outer skin. Inside the ribs the men are laying in the *ceiling*, planks just as thick and strong as the outer shell. At two levels they are fastening *deck clamps*, heavy timber shoulders that will take the butts of the deck framing. The tops of the ribs are trimmed and uprights called *deck stanchions* are fastened between them (these will carry the lighter planking of the *bulwarks* that enclose the main deck).

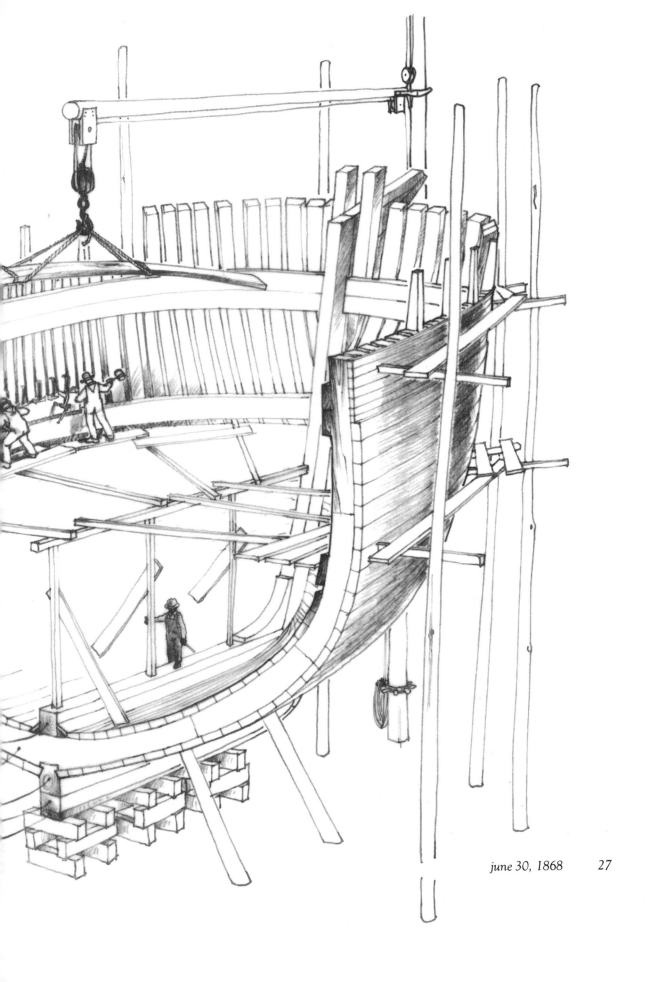

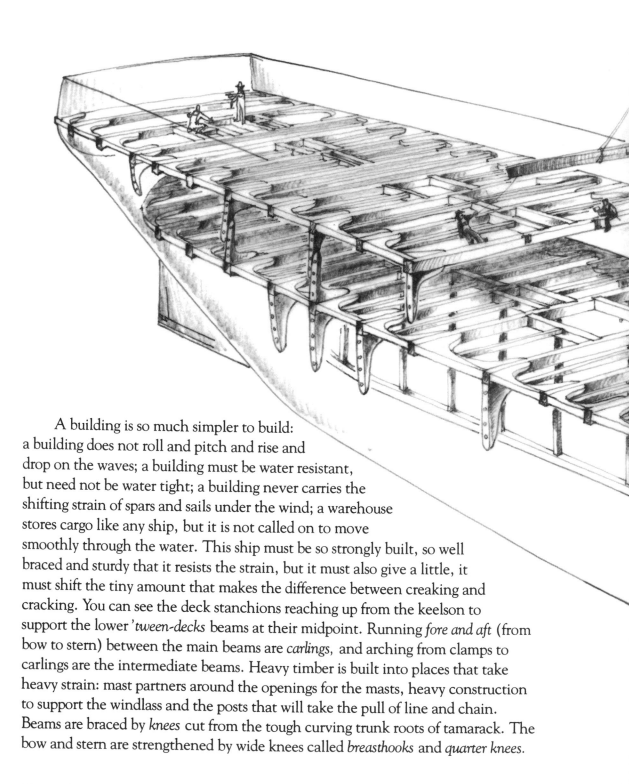

A building is so much simpler to build:
a building does not roll and pitch and rise and
drop on the waves; a building must be water resistant,
but need not be water tight; a building never carries the
shifting strain of spars and sails under the wind; a warehouse
stores cargo like any ship, but it is not called on to move
smoothly through the water. This ship must be so strongly built, so well
braced and sturdy that it resists the strain, but it must also give a little, it
must shift the tiny amount that makes the difference between creaking and
cracking. You can see the deck stanchions reaching up from the keelson to
support the lower *'tween-decks* beams at their midpoint. Running *fore and aft* (from
bow to stern) between the main beams are *carlings,* and arching from clamps to
carlings are the intermediate beams. Heavy timber is built into places that take
heavy strain: mast partners around the openings for the masts, heavy construction
to support the windlass and the posts that will take the pull of line and chain.
Beams are braced by *knees* cut from the tough curving trunk roots of tamarack. The
bow and stern are strengthened by wide knees called *breasthooks* and *quarter knees.*

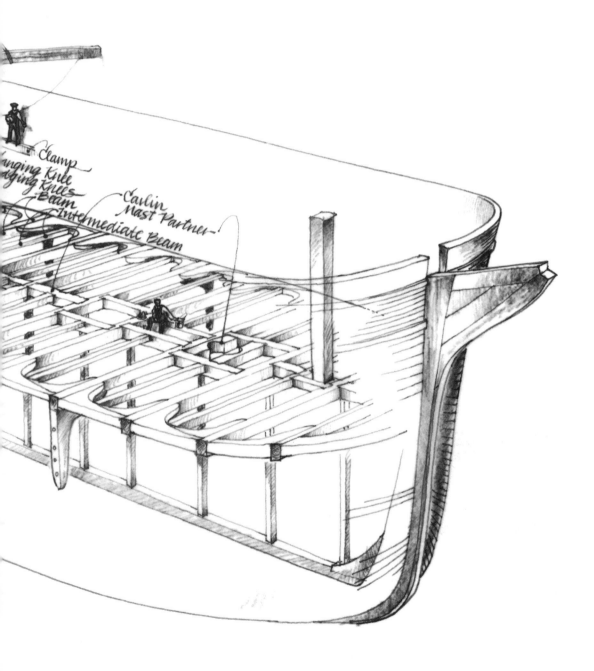

Clamp

Hanging Knee
Hanging Knees
Beam
Intermediate Beam

Carlin
Mast Partner

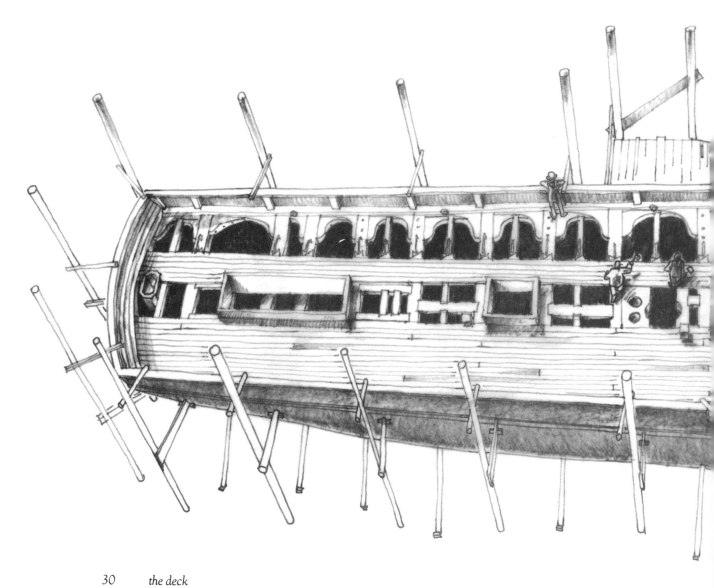

The *hatch coamings* have been fitted. They are boxes built around the deck openings to keep water out. Now the deck is planked around the coamings. Large staples called *dogs* are driven into the beams; with these as a stop, wedges are used to spring the pine planking tightly into place before it is spiked to the beams.

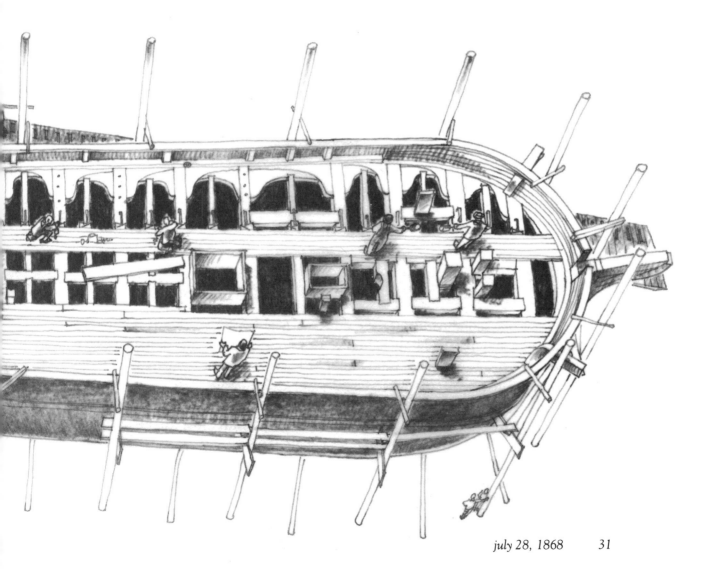

There is one sound peculiar to the shipyard, heard nowhere else. It is music to the shipbuilder and fills the brothers Ingalls with pride. It is the ring of the caulker's mallet. Every space between the planks must be filled to prevent leaking. The caulkers force in twisted hemp (from old tarred rope) called *oakum*. They use a broadbladed *caulking iron* struck with a *caulking mallet* of mesquite wood or live oak, banded on the ends with polished steel. The hull seams are filled with three strands of cotton and oakum, then painted over with red lead paint. The main deck seams are given two strands and filled with hot tar. Almost seven miles of oakum will be driven into the ship, tap by tap. Swinging the gleaming mallets with tarry hands and huge forearms, the caulkers are a special brotherhood.

34   *sheathing*

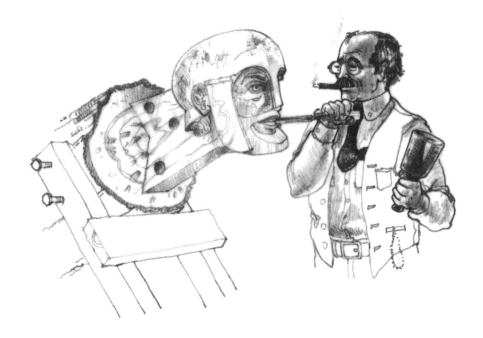

There is a record of an enraged sperm whale attacking a whaleship, ramming it, and sinking it, but one of the ship's main predators is much smaller: the worm. Wood-boring worms eat away at ships surprisingly quickly, and a few months in warm waters would weaken the ship beyond repair if it were not protected by a sheathing of copper from the keel to the water line.

The oaken planking is covered with pitch, then a layer of felt, over which carpenters fit a sheathing of thin white pine. Finally the hull below the water line is encased in metal—copper or an alloy—which will turn away worms and discourage other marine growth.

the launching

It is time to launch this ship. She is not ready for sea, but she is ready for the Acushnet River. The carpenters have been busy on her deck, fitting her out. The brothers Ingalls are pacing nervously, and even the stolid Knowlton seems to be chewing a little heavily on his cigar. The *ways* (slides) are greased and as soon as the *dogs* (wooden braces) are knocked away she will slide back into the river. There is still a lot to be done, but her identity is clear: across her stern in fresh gold leaf is a proud name, *Ulysses.*

On the foredeck Albert and John Ingalls shake hands with Percival Knowlton, with carpenters and yardmen. The Ingallses say a prayer, Knowlton breaks a bottle of black rum over the Samson post, the dogs go flying, the slides screech and smoke as weight and friction set the grease afire, a wave from the stern, a gentle settling, and *Ulysses* is afloat.

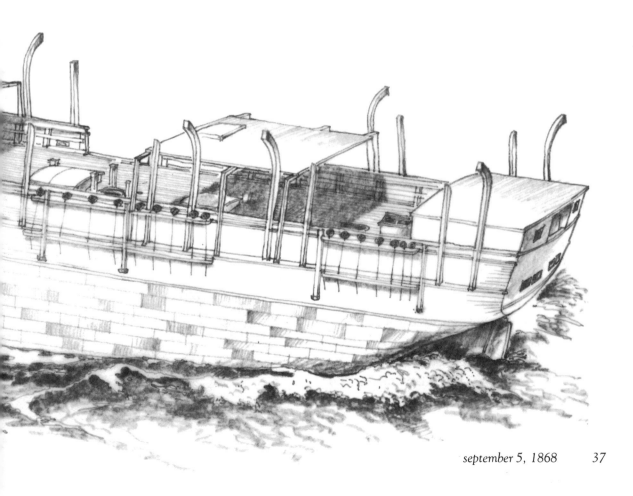

september 5, 1868   37

Part of the wealth of the New World, of America when the English and French and Spanish discovered it, was in her enormous spruce trees. Towering and straight, they were perfect for ships' spars and masts. The trees for this ship's mast have been floated down from Maine, kept in the dirty backwater by the sewage outflow (where worms will not live to bore into them), and hoisted up into the spar shop. First they are roughed out, adzed to a general size with flat faces, and then they are turned on a spar lathe or planed with spar planes, smooth and round.

The foremast, mainmast, and mizzenmast are lifted onto the main deck and swayed down through with shear legs to rest on the keelson—each with a silver coin under its butt, just for luck. The rest of the spars—the topmasts, topgallant masts, and the yards—will be on the dock, waiting for the riggers.

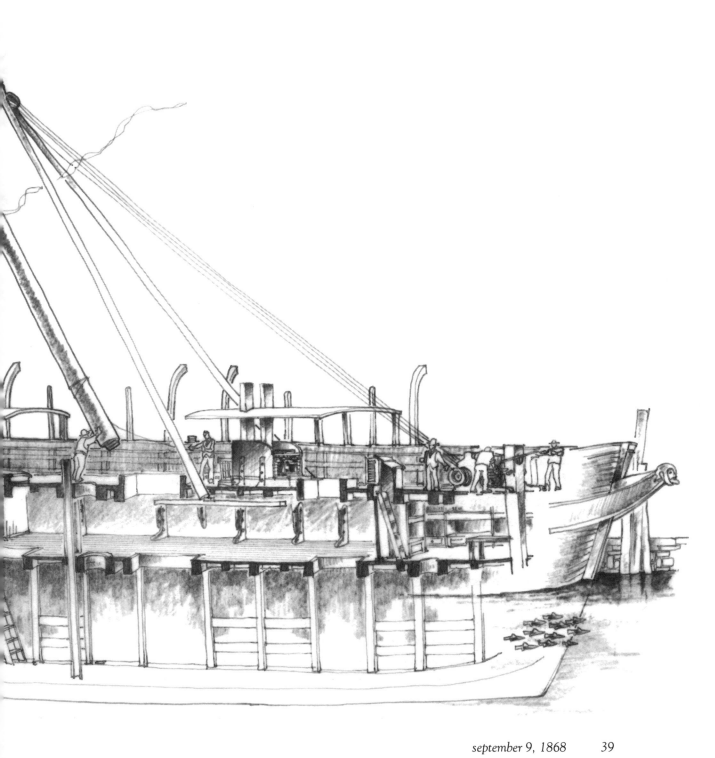

Belowdecks the carpenters are fitting out the *fo'c'sle* (forecastle) forward, where the sailors will live; the living quarters aft for the mates and boatsteerers (harpooneers) and cook; and the elegant cabin for the captain.

Boss Pogany and his crew of riggers are swarming over the ship this week. Their business is tension: they are stretching tarred hemp line until it is "bar taut," holding the slender masts rigidly in place. From the chain plates at the sides of the ship the *shrouds* reach up to brace the masts from side to side. *Stays* brace them fore and aft. When the masts are secure the *topmasts* are rigged above them, and further up the *tapgallant masts* are rigged at a dizzy height. Between the shrouds the riggers have *bent on* (attached) small line that will serve as ladders—the *ratlines*. The *jibboom* is run out on the *bowsprit* and its heavy rigging is set up. The ship will have to be tuned like a guitar . . . a little more tension on the starboard mizzen-topmast shrouds, slack off on the main-topgallant stay, tighter on the martingale stay. Boss Pogany chews his mustache as he sways back and forth in the lookout's perch on the fore-topgallant mast, eyeing the set of the masts and feeling the tension in the shrouds. His men scamper in the rigging below like monkeys in the forest canopy, hoisting up the yards on their *halyards* and setting up the *braces* that will control them (and the sails on them, and the ship, and the voyage).

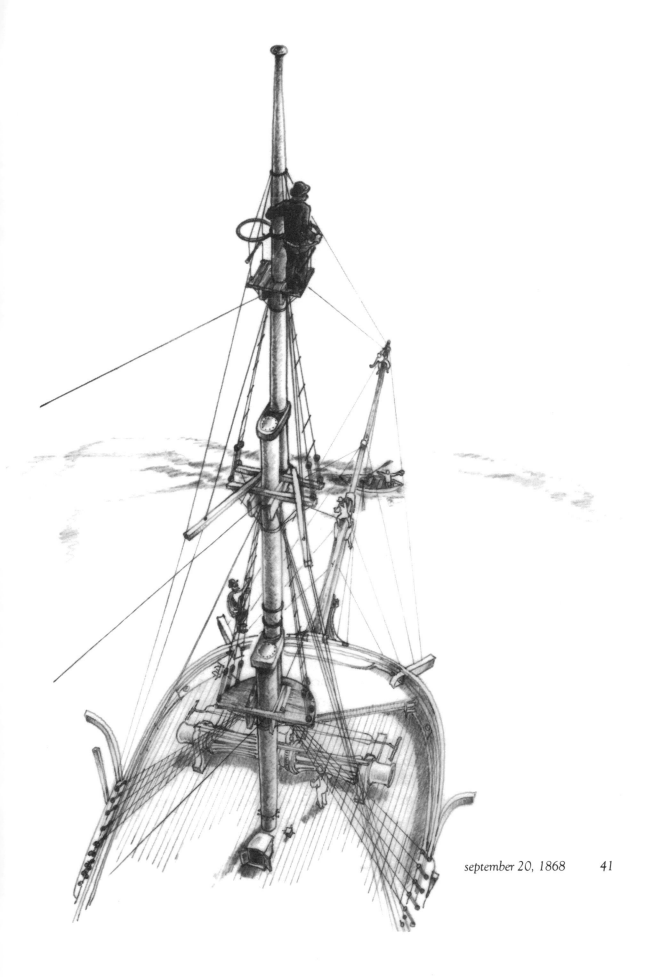

The sail loft on Front Street in New Bedford is cool and airy, even on a hot day. The half-open skylights fill up the broad space with light, which catches the spotless, varnished floor (for laying out sails) and the fresh white canvas. The sailmakers sit quietly in their aprons, stitching the heavy cloth with triangular sail needles and palms. (A *palm* is a piece of leather fitted to the palm for protection and equipped with a metal slug for pushing the needle through the cloth.) In a suit of sails for *Ulysses* there are hundreds of thousands of stitches, eleven thousand square feet of canvas, and miles of thread with easily forty pounds of beeswax on it.

Heavy wagons will line up under the loft doors to receive the sails, spare canvas, and thread, for few of these sails will last the three- or four-year voyage that *Ulysses* can expect.

The forges of the shipsmiths have been hot for weeks. Iron is being pounded into hundreds of essential shapes. Anchors, eyebolts, hinges, hangers, bands, braces,

everything of metal. Both anchors, almost a ton of iron, are forged here, and all the *whalecraft* (harpoons, lances, cutting spades, blubber hooks, skimming baskets, all that touches the whale or its parts).

The blockmaker has been at work, too. His wagon has delivered small signal halyard blocks, the massive cutting-in blocks (*blocks* are what landsmen call pulleys), deadeyes, sheaves for the davits, and another wagon full of blocks for handling yards and sails.

The pumpmaker has installed his wares. The pump tubes and rocker arms are in place around the mainmast.

The cooper has already received his first order for barrels that will hold whale oil. They are waiting in his warehouse, stored in knocked-down bundles called *shooks*.

The ship is almost ready.

Tonight John Ingalls is restless. After supper he walks down the streets of New Bedford to the docks, and out onto the pier where *Ulysses* lies. Seated on a granite block is Mr. Percival Knowlton, smoking one of his black cigars in the twilight. Ingalls sits down beside him and they gaze at the ship, their ship. Whose ship? No one owns her as she lies quiet in the dim light. Ingalls might say she was God's, Knowlton might say that the sea owned her, and there would not be enough difference in the two answers to argue about. After some time they speak casually of her new captain, of her mates and her boatsteerers, of her crew, cooper, carpenter, and, most important to the voyage, her cook. They fall into silence again and watch the darkness gather in her rigging.

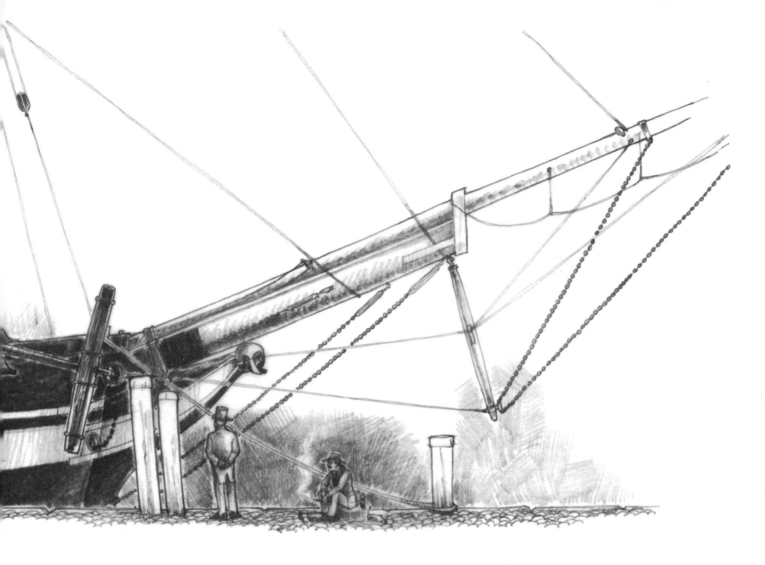

In her oak belly, stowed down scientifically, are 100 barrels of salt beef, 100 of pork, 131 barrels of baking flour, 2000 gallons of molasses, 1119 pounds of coffee, 24,000 cigars, 39 pecks of salt, 172 pounds of nutmeg, 36 pounds of ginger, 319 pounds of tea, 864 buttons, 3 dozen suspenders, every need for thirty men for four years.

John Ingalls mentions that he and his brother look forward to a fine season, and that they are considering sending *Ulysses* to the Arctic grounds if she is successful in the tropic sperm fishery. Mr. Knowlton disagrees. He believes that the ice of the Arctic is more dangerous than the counting houses of New Bedford believe, that *Ulysses* was designed and built for the southern fishery. They fall into silence again. The cigar end glows. They agree on one matter: there is a trace of autumn in the air tonight, just a trace. Mr. Ingalls takes his leave and starts back toward his house on the hill. As he looks back he can just see the red spot of the cigar end in the dark.

In fifteen years *Ulysses* will be caught in an early freeze inside the pack ice of the Bering Strait with sixty-two other whaleships, a third of the New Bedford fleet. Her captain and crew will escape with the others across the ice to three whaleships outside the pack. Within the season the oak timbers from Acushnet, Mattapoisett, Tinkhamtown, and Rochester will be crushed, the ship will sink, and long after the cordage and canvas have melted away, the hull and the almost indestructible wrought iron anchors will lie on the dark, bare bottom of the Arctic Sea. They lie there now.

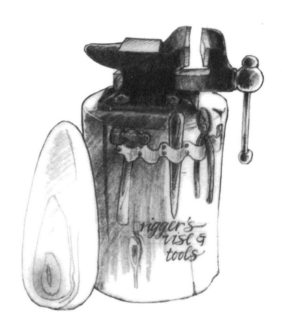

This book was set in Goudy Old Style, 12/15, by Berkeley Typographers, Inc. The running feet are 10/12 Goudy Old Style italic. The display type is a Morgan Press antique wooden face set by The Composing Room of Boston.
The drawings are done in Pelikan plastics ink diluted with snow water, and in fourteen grades of graphite pencil on Herculene film.